Three Little Kittens

Retold by STEVEN ANDERSON

Illustrated by DOREEN MARTS

CANTATA
LEARNING

WWW.CANTATALEARNING.COM

CANTATA LEARNING

Published by Cantata Learning
1710 Roe Crest Drive
North Mankato, MN 56003
www.cantatalearning.com

Library of Congress Control Number: 2015932795
Anderson, Steven
    Three Little Kittens / retold by Steven Anderson; Illustrated by Doreen Marts
    Series: Sing-along Animal Songs
    Audience: Ages: 3–8; Grades: PreK–3
    Summary: In this classic song, learn about opposites as the three little kittens
lose their mittens.
    ISBN: 978-1-63290-371-6 (library binding/CD)
    ISBN: 978-1-63290-502-4 (paperback/CD)
    ISBN: 978-1-63290-532-1 (paperback)
    1. Stories in rhyme. 2. Cats (Kittens)—fiction. 3. Opposites—fiction.

Book design and art direction, Tim Palin Creative
Editorial direction, Flat Sole Studio
Music direction, Elizabeth Draper
Music arranged and produced by Steven C Music

Printed in the United States of America in North Mankato, Minnesota.
122015   0326CGS16

ACCESS THE MUSIC!

SCAN CODE WITH MOBILE APP

CANTATALEARNING.COM

The three little kittens just want to go outside and play. But what will their mother say when they can't find their mittens? Will the three kittens get to have some fun?

To find out, turn the page and sing along!

The three little kittens
lost their mittens,
and they began to cry.

"Oh, Mother dear,
we sadly fear
that our mittens are lost."

"What? Lost your mittens,
you silly kittens!
Now you can't go outside."

Meow. Meow. Meow.

"You must find your mittens."

The three little kittens
found their mittens,
and they began to shout.

"Oh, Mother dear,
see here, see here.
Let's go out
and play!"

The three little kittens
put on their mittens,
and they went out to play.

"Oh, Mother dear,
we greatly fear
we've dirtied our mittens."

"What? Dirtied your mittens,
you silly kittens!"
The kittens began to sigh.

Meow. Meow. Meow.

"You must wash your mittens."

The three little kittens
went to wash their mittens,
and they began to cry.

"Oh, Mother dear,
do you not hear?
Now our mittens are wet!"

"What? You have wet mittens,
you silly kittens!"
The kittens began to sigh.

Meow. Meow. Meow.

"You must dry your mittens."

The three little kittens
hung up their mittens
and waited for them to dry.

Then they smelled a rat close by
and forgot all about their mittens.

Meow. Meow. Meow.

SONG LYRICS
Three Little Kittens

The three little kittens
lost their mittens,
and they began to cry.

"Oh, Mother dear,
we sadly fear
that our mittens are lost."

"What? Lost your mittens,
you silly kittens!
Now you can't go outside."

Meow. Meow. Meow.

"You must find your mittens."

The three little kittens
found their mittens,
and they began to shout.

"Oh, Mother dear,
see here, see here.
Let's go out and play!"

The three little kittens
put on their mittens,
and they went out to play.

"Oh, Mother dear,
we greatly fear
we've dirtied our mittens."

"What? Dirtied your mittens,
you silly kittens!"
The kittens began to sigh.

Meow. Meow. Meow.

"You must wash your mittens."

The three little kittens
went to wash their mittens,
and they began to cry.

"Oh, Mother dear,
do you not hear?
Now our mittens are wet!"

"What? You have wet mittens,
you silly kittens!"
The kittens began to sigh.

Meow. Meow. Meow.

"You must dry your mittens."

The three little kittens
hung up their mittens
and waited for them to dry.

Then they smelled a rat close by
and forgot all about their mittens.

Meow. Meow. Meow.

Three Little Kittens

Ska
Steven C Music

Verse 2
"What? Lost your mittens, you silly kittens!
Now you can't go outside."
Meow. Meow. Meow. "You must find your mittens."

Verse 3
The three little kittens found their mittens,
and they began to shout.
"Oh, Mother dear, see here, see here.
Let's go out and play!"

Verse 4
The three little kittens put on their mittens,
and they went out to play.
"Oh, Mother dear, we greatly fear
we've dirtied our mittens."

Verse 5
"What? Dirtied your mittens, you silly kittens!"
The kittens began to sigh.
Meow. Meow. Meow. "You must wash your mittens."

Verse 6
The three little kittens went to wash their mittens,
and they began to cry.
"Oh, Mother dear, do you not hear?
Now our mittens are wet!"

Verse 7
"What? You have wet mittens, you silly kittens!"
The kittens began to sigh.
Meow. Meow. Meow. "You must dry your mittens."

Verse 8
The three little kittens hung up their mittens
and waited for them to dry.
Then they smelled a rat close by
and forgot all about their mittens.
Meow. Meow. Meow.

GUIDED READING ACTIVITIES

1. Look at the kittens. What colors are they? What is your favorite color?

2. What season is it in this story? What season is it where you are?

3. Fold a piece of paper in half. Then, with a crayon or marker, and keeping your fingers together, trace around your fingers and thumb. You just drew a mitten! Cut it out, and you will have two mittens. Now make designs on your new pair of mittens.

TO LEARN MORE

Bader, Bonnie. *Kit-kit-kittens*. New York: Penguin Young Readers, 2015.

Galdone, Paul. *Three Little Kittens: A Folk Tale Classic*. Boston: Houghton Mifflin Harcourt, 2011.

Olson, Bethany. *Baby Cats*. Minneapolis: Bellwether Media, 2014.

Weidner, Teri. *Three Little Kittens*. Mankato, MN: Child's World, 2011.